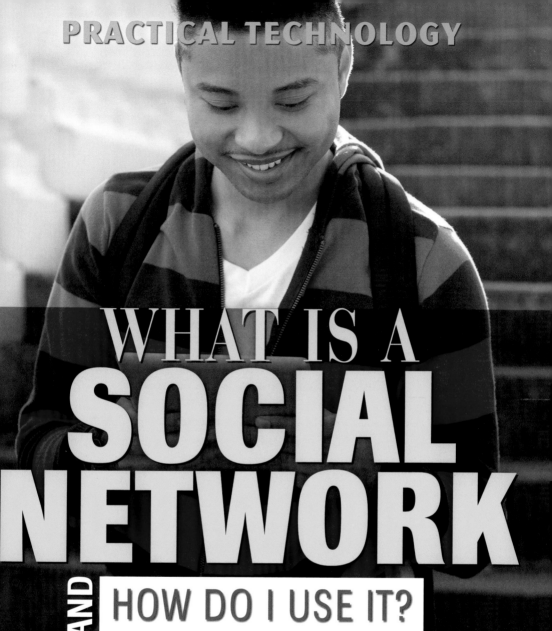

WHAT IS A SOCIAL NETWORK AND HOW DO I USE IT?

LEON GRAY

Britannica
Educational Publishing

IN ASSOCIATION WITH

ROSEN
EDUCATIONAL SERVICES

Published in 2014 by Britannica Educational Publishing (a trademark of Encyclopædia Britannica, Inc.) in association with The Rosen Publishing Group, Inc.
29 East 21st Street, New York, NY 10010

Distributed exclusively by Rosen Publishing.
To see additional Britannica Educational Publishing titles, go to rosenpublishing.com

First Edition

Britannica Educational Publishing
J.E. Luebering: Director, Core Reference Group
Anthony L. Green: Editor, Compton's by Britannica

Rosen Publishing
Hope Lourie Killcoyne: Executive Editor
Nelson Sá: Art Director

Library of Congress Cataloging-in-Publication Data

Gray, Leon, 1974-
What is a social network and how do I use it? / Leon Gray. — First edition.
    pages cm. — (Practical technology)
Audience: Grade 5 to 8.
Includes bibliographical references and index.
ISBN 978-1-62275-075-7 (library bound) — ISBN 978-1-62275-076-4 (paperback) — ISBN 978-1-62275-291-1 (6 pack)
1. Online social networks—Juvenile literature. I. Title.
HM742.G73 2014
006.7'54—dc23

                                        2013027171

Manufactured in the United States of America

CONTENTS

Introduction   4

CHAPTER 1   NETWORKING BASICS   6

CHAPTER 2   HOW TO USE SOCIAL NETWORKS   14

CHAPTER 3   TYPES OF SOCIAL NETWORK SITES   20

CHAPTER 4   SOCIAL NETWORK SAFETY   32

CHAPTER 5   SOCIAL NETWORK FUTURE   38

Start Networking   44
Glossary   46
For More Information   47
Index   48

INTRODUCTION

Social networking is a way of using a computer or smartphone to talk to other people. Any form of communication with a group of people is an example of a social network. In that sense, nothing is new. Our ancestors made connections with family, friends, and neighboring villages, but they did not use computers.

Social networks, sometimes called social media, are part of popular culture. As long as you follow a few simple rules, they can be a source of fun. They also have a more serious side. For example, social media have helped with disaster relief and to bring about political change.

Facebook and Twitter are perhaps two of the best-known examples of social media. However, there are many others, for example, YouTube, Myspace, and Instagram. This book will give you the information you need to start using social networks safely and effectively.

You can have great fun keeping in touch with people using Twitter and other social networking sites.

CHAPTER 1

NETWORKING BASICS

Social networks are present in almost every area of our lives—they are all the connections that we form with other people on a daily basis.

MAKING A MAP

Put simply, social networks are the relationships that connect people. These relationships are defined by our family, friends, school, hobbies, work, and much more. If you tried to sit down and map all these connections, you would probably not get very far. Social networking websites make the process much easier by mapping them out.

SOCIAL EXPERIMENT

As long ago as 1929, a Hungarian author named Frigyes Karinthy (1887–1938) wrote about communication becoming easier as the modern world progressed.

In 1961, a U.S. psychologist named Stanley Milgram (1933–1984) decided to test out Karinthy's idea in a process called "six degrees of separation."

Six Degrees of Separation

Milgram sent 160 packages to random people in Omaha, Nebraska. He instructed them to mail the packages to someone with whom they were on first name terms. The recipients would do the same, with the aim of getting the package to a named person in Boston in the fewest moves possible. The average number of mailings was six, which led to the idea of "six degrees of separation." Milgram's experiment showed that there is an increasing degree of interconnectivity in the modern age.

Social networking sites make it much easier to keep in touch with family and friends.

Networking by Nature

Social networks are important because they provide resources in the form of information, relationships, and community. These combined resources are called "social capital."

Enhancing Social Capital

Research suggests that social networks enhance social capital. They allow users to target people with shared interests. Through social media, we can establish and maintain relationships with people we might not normally come into contact with. Communication is quick, and we can talk to different people at once. Before the Internet, this type of communication was difficult, especially between people who lived far apart.

Practical Technology

People are social animals by nature, so the idea of social networking is not new or unusual. In a practical sense, it helps people keep in touch with family and a wider circle of friends. It might also provide quick access to information and ideas, enabling users to write a better homework assignment or prepare for an important project, for example.

REAL RELATIONSHIPS

Some people argue that online social networks endanger real-life relationships. Ultimately this could threaten a person's overall social capital. It is a good idea to maintain a balance between relationships with people online and in person.

Using social networking sites can become a problem if it starts to interfere with your real life.

CIRCLE OF TIES

Social networks consist of strong and weak ties. Strong ties include family members and close friends. A weak tie could be someone you met at summer camp a couple of years ago.

STRONG TIES

Strong ties are hard to maintain because they take up time. You need to stay in regular contact to maintain the close relationship.

Social networking sites are great for keeping in touch with people, but they are no substitute for spending real time with your friends.

Social media is a useful way of maintaining strong ties. This communication could be telling family and friends about an upcoming birthday party or keeping in touch with a relative who lives in a different country. Strong ties take up a lot of time and energy, so there is a limit to how many people you can be so close with at one time.

Weak Ties

Weak ties are limitless. They can include almost anyone you have ever met, from your dentist to someone you once met at a party. Social media sites are an ideal way to keep in touch with people outside your close circle of family and friends.

EXPANDING HORIZONS

Weak ties can become just as important as strong ties. They allow people to expand their social network and find new friends. This can lead to stronger connections and introduce you to ideas and opinions that you might not have otherwise encountered.

New Technology

Before we had automobiles, airplanes, and the Internet, people generally lived in the same town and socialized with the same people. As technology has advanced, our social networks have become much bigger.

Expanding the Network

Many different technologies allow people to expand their social networks. They include traditional telephone calls as well as e-mails, instant messaging (IM), social media, and wireless communication. When all this new technology works together, people are constantly communicating and maintaining their social network.

Social networking can happen just about anywhere using a smartphone.

On the Move

In the recent past, social networking was only possible on the telephone or by e-mail on a desktop computer. Social networking took place in a fixed spot within the home. Today, people use laptops, iPads and other tablets, and smartphones to communicate, so social networking can now happen just about anywhere.

Most social media sites have apps that allow you to chat with other people when you are online.

WATCH WHAT YOU WRITE

IM is the ability to "chat" online. It is very important to remember that some chat happens in real time and can be seen as you type. It is therefore important to think before you write. You could upset someone, or even break the law and end up in a lot of trouble if you write abusive or inflammatory messages.

CHAPTER 2

HOW TO USE SOCIAL NETWORKS

There are more than 300 social networking sites. In this chapter, you can find out about creating a profile, adding information about yourself, and uploading photographs.

Before creating your online profile, seek permission from a responsible adult. Be aware that some social network sites, such as Facebook and Myspace, have a minimum age requirement of 13 or 14 years.

PASSWORD SECURITY

The first thing to think about when creating a profile is choosing a strong password. A combination of letters, numbers, and special characters, such as (*!&), is good. Avoid using your name or date of birth.

SITE RESTRICTIONS

Some sites have restrictions on young people's accounts. For example, they may not assign a private profile to anyone under the age of 16 and may block adults from contacting you without your approval. Respect the restrictions—they are there for your safety.

CREATING A PROFILE

Here is a step-by-step guide to creating a profile:

1. Choose a social networking site. Examples include Facebook, Twitter, and Instagram.
2. Enter the required personal information to sign up. Do not add your phone number or full address.
3. The site will then help you to add friends. Remember, you should connect only with people you know.
4. Expand your profile with information about your hobbies and interests.
5. Add your profile picture or avatar. Most sites allow you to search for a picture on your hard drive. Check with a responsible adult that the image you choose is appropriate.
6. The site will then send a confirmation link e-mail to your e-mail address. Now your profile is complete.

Creating your online profile is easy. Most sites will guide you through the process so you can start to build your social network.

FINDING FRIENDS

Once you have set up your profile, the next step is to search for existing friends and browse for new contacts.

You can invite friends to join your social network by sending them a request via e-mail or directly to their profile. Some sites link into your e-mail account to help with this process.

SEARCH TOOLS

You can also look for new friends on a social networking site. You can search by e-mail address, user name, real name, or even by affiliation to your school or where you live. As more people accept your invitation, you will expand your social network. Remember that some people may not accept your invitation.

PRIVACY MATTERS!

This may seem obvious, but you are more likely to find friends if you use your real name and you fill in your details carefully and honestly. However, you may not want to share your details with everyone on the social network. It is a good idea to make sure your privacy settings are switched on. Any details you input are in the public domain unless you set up these filters correctly.

Once you have added friends to your social network on Facebook, the pictures, links, and other posts that they share will show up on a page called your News Feed. You can change your settings to filter content you wouldn't like to see from the content you would like to appear.

IN THE PICTURE

Your friends may post pictures and link them to your profile. You will need to monitor this. If you think a picture is inappropriate, remove the link from your profile immediately.

EXPANDING YOUR CIRCLE

Once you have added your existing friends to your social network, you can start to expand your circle of friends.

FRIEND OF A FRIEND

A good place to start looking for new friends is through your existing friends' connections. You might want to invite people who share the same interests or like the same music. Social networks are not popularity contests. It does not matter how many friends you make as long as the friends you do make are genuine.

GROUPS AND TAGS

Some social networking sites let you create interest groups, for example, to see if anyone shares the same hobbies or likes the same television programs that you do.

You will expand your circle of friends as you spend more time on social networking sites.

You can also search sites by tags. Tags are bookmarks and links to information, sites, and people. They can be attached to any type of content, such as a photo or video upload.

THE REAL DEAL

Unfortunately, there are people on the Internet who are not whom they claim to be. Accept friend requests only from people you know. Never add a person to your network if you feel he or she may not be trustworthy.

BLOCKING BULLIES

If anyone ever threatens or harasses you on a social networking site, block them immediately and tell a responsible adult. Remember, you can block anybody you want to, at any time.

CHAPTER 3

TYPES OF SOCIAL NETWORK SITES

As well as creating a profile, building a list of friends, and adding new contacts, many social networking sites share common features.

Adding to Your Home Page

Most sites allow users to upload digital photos and video clips. They also provide the user with the opportunity to comment on what they are doing and how they feel. This usually takes the form of a "blog" entry or "status update."

Feeds

User profiles may also have a "feed," which displays comments from friends on the network. Some sites have more specific features, which include the ability to create groups of users who live in the same area or who share common interests.

Special Interests

Some social networks have developed into sites for users with a specific interest. For example, Myspace is a platform for music fans to keep up to date with news about their favorite artists.

You can use social networks to invite friends
to play your favorite online games.

GAMING

Some social networking sites allow you to
play games against people with whom you are
connected. Facebook, Myspace, and Twitter
have free games. These are often grouped into
sections, for example, action games, puzzles,
and strategy games.

AD SPACE

Before social networking sites appeared,
advertising an event, such as a garage sale
or a music gig, required a lot of footwork to put
up posters in the local area. Social networking
sites allow you to advertise these events for free
and to target the people who are most likely
to attend—your family and friends!

Facebook

Facebook is the world's most popular social networking site. It has more than one billion active users and this number grows every day.

Mark Zuckerberg and some friends founded Facebook in February 2004. They developed it to connect the students at Harvard University. Facebook spread to other universities, then to high schools, and eventually to anyone over the age of 13. Very quickly, Facebook overtook rivals such as Myspace to become the world's most popular social media site.

New Developments

In March 2012, Facebook launched its App Center to sell applications for the iPhone, Android, and mobile web users. Other developments include video calling using Skype, messaging, the "Like" button, movie ratings, and recommendations.

Too Much Time

Some critics believe that people spend too much time using Facebook. However, others argue that using social networks is not a problem as long as users maintain a good balance between the time they spend online and offline.

THE NETWORK BIO

Mark Zuckerberg was born in New York in 1984. He developed Facebook while he was a computer science student at Harvard University. He launched the site in 2004. By May 2012, Facebook was valued at an incredible $104 billion.

Facebook has quickly grown to become the world's most widely used social networking site.

TWITTER

Twitter is a social networking site that allows users to post short messages, called "tweets." When Jack Dorsey first came up with the idea for Twitter in 2006, he envisaged a site on which users posted tweets to tell other people what they were thinking or doing at the time.

FOLLOWING ON TWITTER

Twitter allows people to follow other users and read their tweets. You can follow other Twitter users without becoming friends, but they might not reply to your tweets. You can also post digital images and short video clips. However, age restrictions apply to video posts.

In June 2013, Justin Bieber had more than 40 million Twitter followers. He is one of the most followed celebrities.

THE NETWORK BIO

Jack Dorsey was born in St. Louis, Missouri, in 1976. He came up with the idea for Twitter while he was a student at New York University. He launched the site in 2006. Twitter became a voice for many people around the world, including famous people such as President Obama, who has more than 31,000,000 followers.

FOLLOW THE FEED

Twitter is popular because people can follow their favorite celebrities. When these stars post a tweet, it appears in your Twitter feed. If you follow a lot of people, you can use Twitter's free app to help you manage and group the feed.

TWEET CAREFULLY

Remember that tweets are posted in real time and they are in the public domain unless you activate the privacy settings. You need to think carefully about what you tweet. Do not post offensive or inappropriate messages.

COMMUNITY SITES

Almost all social networking sites can be defined as community sites because they all attempt to widen a user's circle of friends. However, there are social networking sites that try to target users with similar interests and backgrounds. These are community sites.

CONNECTING PEOPLE

Black Planet and Asian Avenue are sites that target people who share the same ethnic origin. Myspace connects people who share a similar interest in music. LinkedIn is community site for people in the working world.

JOIN THE COMMUNITY

There are many community sites. Here are just a couple of examples:
- Dweeber encourages students to collaborate on their homework assignments and solve problems.
- deviantART is a community site that allows users to showcase works of art.

Some social networks help connect people with similar backgrounds, such as ethnic origin, or interests, such as music.

MEDIA-SHARING SITES

Media-sharing sites allow users to upload digital content such as photos and video clips. Anyone can visit these sites and view the material, but you have to become a member to upload your own content.

Most social networking sites allow users to upload photos and videos. Media-sharing sites are specifically devoted to these tasks. Once you have become a member, media-sharing sites work like any other social network. You can invite people to become a friend, and they will then be listed on your contacts page.

YOUTUBE

One of the most popular video-sharing sites is YouTube. It allows users to upload, view, and share a range of video content, such as music videos, movie trailers, television clips, and amateur video footage.

INSTAGRAM

Instagram is a popular online photo-sharing site and social networking service. It allows users to upload photos and use special filters to change the style of the images. Many celebrities have Instagram profiles, giving users a glimpse into their private lives.

SHARING CONTENT

Here are the basic steps to sharing content on a media-sharing site.

1. Create an account on a site such as Instagram or YouTube.
2. Follow the instructions to upload your digital photos or video files.
3. Share the address to publicize your content, and embed it in other web pages to give others easy access.

Remember that anyone can view your photos and videos. Always keep your personal details private. For example, do not post pictures that show the outside of your home or your school.

YouTube - Broadcast Yourself.

www.youtube.com/

You Tube

YouTube is a popular social network that is used to share videos. Viewers can post comments about the content shown there.

There are hundreds of social networking sites on the Internet. They are a great way to connect with other people who share your special interests.

OTHER SOCIAL NETWORKS

One current trend in social networks is sites with a specific focus, such as bookmarking, blogging, music, and sport.

BOOKMARKING

Social bookmarking sites, such as Pinterest, allow you to tag websites and information that you find useful or enjoyable. They act as virtual libraries and store the sites as bookmarks so you can access them whenever you want to.

Blogs

Blogs are online journals. People write about their lives, thoughts, and feelings on blogs. Many sites offer free services. Check out WordPress (www.wordpress.com) and Google Blogger (www.blogger.com) for details.

Sports Sites

Strava is an app that works with GPS-enabled devices. The app tracks and records activities such as cycle rides and training runs. After the activity, users can then analyze the results and compare them with other athletes.

JOIN THE COMMUNITY

There are many specialist networking sites you can connect with. Here are just a few examples:
- **Elftown** is a network aimed at science fiction and fantasy fans.
- **Flixster** is a community where users share movie reviews and ratings.
- **gamerDNA** focuses on game playing.
- **WeeWorld** is a fun social network aimed at 10–17 year olds.

Always seek permission from a responsible adult before you sign up at any of these social networking sites.

CHAPTER 4

SOCIAL NETWORK SAFETY

O nce you have signed up at a social networking site, it is surprising how quickly your profile can build up. How can you be sure that this information is kept safe?

BE PRIVATE

You will not want your profile to be read by just anyone, so you need to implement the correct privacy settings. Always read the privacy policy of a social networking site before you agree to join. Ask an adult to help you with this if you find it complicated. If you are not happy with the terms of use, do not join the site.

PRIVACY MATTERS

Almost all social networking sites allow you to block people from accessing your profile, but in many cases, the default, or usual, setting is to allow access to everyone. As a result, you will need to manage your settings to allow only family and friends to access your profile. You should also be able to remove tags on photos and posts if you do not want to be in them.

ONLINE DANGERS

Online dangers include cyberstalking and identity theft. Cyberstalking involves someone using online tools to harass people by posting offensive messages on their profile page. Identity theft is the stealing of private information by criminals to commit fraud.

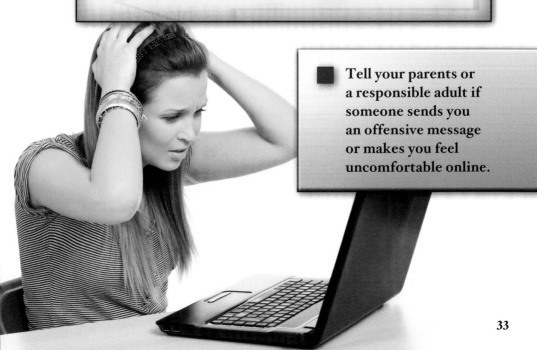

SOCIAL SCREENING

Colleges and universities have been known to search social media sites for information about potential students. This is also true of employers. Never post anything that could be used to harm your reputation—now or in the future.

Tell your parents or a responsible adult if someone sends you an offensive message or makes you feel uncomfortable online.

Cyberbullying is exactly the same as bullying in real life. How would you feel if someone did it to you?

Online Bullying

The popularity of social media sites has led to a new form of bullying, called cyberbullying.

What Is Cyberbullying?

Social media sites make it easy for bullies to pick on people they do not like. Bullies hide behind the Internet and send abusive or threatening messages to upset and intimidate other Internet users. Although this is just name-calling, nonetheless, it is still bullying and it is completely unacceptable.

Trolling and Flaming

"Trolling" and "flaming" are two other names for unwanted, bullying behavior. A troll is someone who posts rude messages in an online community. The main aim of trolling is to provoke a response. The best way to deal with trolls is to ignore their abusive messages. Flaming, or bashing, is an insulting and hostile online conversation between two people.

BEATING THE BULLIES

Here are some basic rules for dealing with trolls, flamers, and other cyberbullies:

- Never respond to an abusive message.
- Always tell a responsible adult if you are a victim of cyberbullying.
- Tell the police if you think the law has been broken.
- Keep a copy of any abusive messages and record the date and the time they were sent.
- You can make your social network profile temporarily inactive or delete it altogether if necessary.
- Ignore the bully, but take action. People are there to help you, so tell someone about the problem as soon as you can.

Spending too much time on social networking sites can lead to problems in the real world. It is unhealthy if, for example, using networking sites becomes more important than doing schoolwork.

Social Network Addict

Social networking sites should widen our circle of friends and keep users better connected. However, some critics argue that they have exactly the opposite effect.

Forgetting Your Friends

By focusing too much attention on virtual friends, users may run the risk of harming the in-person relationships they have with others. Some critics argue that people are becoming addicted to social networking sites.

Self Obsession

Today, it sometimes seems that everyone knows everything about everybody. People write about and post photographs of themselves on social media sites, for everyone to see. Doing so can lead to people competing with each other to reveal more about their lives on the Internet.

BETTER BALANCE

Remember that your online profile is only one part of your life. Always try to make time for lots of different activities—both online and offline—to have a rich, rewarding life.

CHAPTER 5

SOCIAL NETWORK FUTURE

Today, more people access networking sites on the go using smartphones and tablets. This is known as mobile social networking.

GPS On Phones

Social networking sites have responded to this new trend with some great developments. These include apps that make use of GPS. FourSquare, Instagram, and Facebook offer location-based services (LBS) as part of a mobile social network. LBS allows you, for instance, to meet nearby friends without having to call to find out where they are!

Augmented Reality

Augmented reality is a way of putting computer-generated content into a real environment. Practical applications include placing images of a building on its archeological remains, teachers putting photos directly onto students' computer screens, and televised sports that superimpose images onto the field. This technology enables you to create videos that mix real and cartoon imagery.

APPLICATIONS OF LBS

Here some examples of useful LBS you may use:
- Navigation to a specified address.
- Recommending an event in a specific place.
- Recommending local services, such as the nearest coffee shop or gas station.
- Location-based gaming, such as geocaching and geodashing.
- Letting your friends and family know where you are.

Gamers use GPS to find geocaches, which are a little like treasures.

Barack Obama used his Twitter account in the 2008 election to inform and interact with voters. He still regularly tweets to communicate with the American public.

SOCIAL MEDIA MARKETING

Many people use Facebook and other social networks to post data about their likes and dislikes. Businesses are tapping into this trend and using social media as a way to effectively market to specific audiences. Many companies currently use the wealth of information on social media sites to launch online marketing campaigns. They can use this information to target exactly the right people for their products.

Divided Opinion

Some people object to the way in which companies use personal information to target advertising at people. They believe that this violates the privacy policies of the sites. They argue that companies should not be allowed to target young people. Be aware of targeted advertising, and always research and consider a range of options before committing to a product or service.

Not Always for Profit

Social media marketing activities are not always driven by business objectives. In 2011, an anti-bullying documentary called *Bully* was launched on social media sites. It raised awareness among students and teenagers.

BUILDING CUSTOMER LOYALTY

One of the main aims of many businesses is to encourage people to interact with them. Businesses sometimes use social networks to encourage users to visit their site, play games, and rate products. Through this engagement, businesses hope to build a loyal customer base.

FUTURE TRENDS

Ten years ago social networking was virtually unknown. Today, it is a growing phenomenon. Imagine what it might be like in ten years' time.

KEEPING IT CLOSE

Future trends may include a rise in private social networks. These attempt to make social networking less public. Specialist sites may also become more popular. Sites of particular interest may create more meaningful networks.

JOINING UP

Another likely development may be integrated services joining different platforms—social media, apps, and websites—into one interface. An Application Programming Interface (API) allows different platforms to communicate.

NEW TRENDS

Other social networking developments include:
- Cloud computing to allow people to store information more securely.
- Gesture and voice control technologies.
- Online commerce to allow people to shop more securely.

Social networking is a relatively recent development, but it looks set to play an important role in our lives for many decades to come.

START NETWORKING

The rise of social networking sites has been phenomenal. As long as you are aware of the dangers and take the necessary measures to stay safe, there is much to explore and enjoy.

ASKING QUESTIONS

Before you engage in any social networking, consider what you are going to write. Whatever you post online will be available for people to see and could be accessible for many years. Make sure that your communications with people do not end up being a source of embarrassment or misery in years to come.

Many people use smartphones to connect with people, making it quicker and easier to use social networks.

TOP TIPS FOR USING SOCIAL NETWORKS

1. Get permission from a responsible adult before joining a social network.
2. Stay safe. If anyone threatens or harasses you on a social networking site, block them immediately and tell a responsible adult.
3. Watch what you write. You cannot change a comment once it has been posted, so be sure you will not regret what you have written.
4. Choose your privacy settings wisely—you may not want everybody viewing your profile.
5. Read the privacy policy. If you are not happy with the terms of use—such as who, if anyone, the site will share your profile information with—do not join the site.
6. Keep your personal details private. Remember that unless you change the privacy settings, anyone can view any photos and videos you upload to media-sharing sites such as YouTube.
7. Balance your online and offline activities. Do not let social networking interfere with your offline life.
8. Manage your digital impression. Never post information or photos that could be used to harm your reputation—now or in the future.
9. Never respond to abusive messages. If possible, block the person who wrote them and tell a responsible adult.
10. Last, but not least: have fun!

app Short for application software—a program that tells a computer or electronic device to do something.

augmented reality Technology used to put computer-generated images in a real-world environment.

avatar Something, such as a badge or cartoon character, used to represent an online user.

blogging Using an online journal, called a blog (a contraction of the words web and log).

circle of ties The strong and weak ties in your network.

cloud computing Using and storing files over the Internet.

community sites Specialized social media sites that focus on certain themes.

cyberbullying Using the Internet to bully someone.

cyberstalking Using the Internet to harass someone.

flaming An insulting and hostile conversation between two people on the Internet.

geocaching A game in which players use GPS receivers to search for hidden treasure, called a geocache.

geodashing A game in which players use GPS receivers to find and visit "dashpoints" around the world.

GPS Short for Global Positioning System—satellites that communicate with radio receivers to calculate someone or something's geographical position.

instant messaging (IM) Sending messages on the Internet in real time.

location-based services (LBS) Software that makes use of GPS receivers to provide geographical information about a person or object.

privacy settings The tools that keep your online life private.

public domain Something that is not under copyright, so anyone can use it.

Skype An online application that allows you to make video calls, instant message, or chat with contacts.

smartphone A cell phone that has computing abilities such as Internet connectivity.

social capital The benefits gained from your circle of friends.

trolling Posting rude messages to an online community.

tweets 140-character messages that are posted on the social networking site Twitter.

upload To post computer files to the Internet.

Books

Gilbert, Sara. *Built for Success: The Story of Facebook*. Mankato, MN: Creative Paperbacks, 2013.

Linde, Barbara M. *Safe Social Networking* (Cyberspace Survival Guide). New York, NY: Gareth Stevens, 2012.

Meyer, Jared. *Making Friends: The Art of Social Networking in Life and Online* (Communicating With Confidence). New York, NY: Rosen Publishing Group, 2011.

Nelson, Drew. *Dealing with Cyberbullies* (Cyberspace Survival Guide). New York, NY: Gareth Stevens, 2012.

Schwartz, Heather. *Safe Social Networking* (Fact Finders). North Mankato, MN: Capstone Press, 2013.

Websites

Due to the changing nature of Internet links, Rosen Publishing has developed an online list of websites related to the subject of this book. This site is updated regularly. Please use this link to access the list:

http://www.rosenlinks.com/ptech/netw

advertising 21, 41
Application Programming Interface
   (API) 42
App Center 22
apps 13, 31, 38, 42
Asian Avenue 26
augmented reality 38

Black Planet 26
blog 20, 30, 31

circle of ties 10–11
cloud computing 42
community sites 26
cyberbullying 34–35
cyberstalking 33

deviantART 26
Dorsey, Jack 24, 25
Dweeber 26

e-mails 12, 13, 15, 16

Facebook 5, 14, 15, 21, 22-23, 38, 40
feeds 20, 25
flaming 35
FourSquare 38

gaming 21, 39
geocaching 39
geodashing 39
Google Blogger, 31
GPS 31, 38, 39

identity theft 33
Instagram 5, 15, 28, 29, 38
instant messaging (IM) 12, 13
Internet 8, 12, 19, 30, 34, 37

Karinthy, Frigyes 6

laptops 13
LinkedIn 26
location-based services (LBS) 38, 39

marketing 40–41
Milgram, Stanley 6, 7
mobile social networking 38
Myspace 5, 14, 20, 21, 22, 26

Obama, President Barack 25, 40

password 14
photographs 14, 19, 20, 28, 29, 32, 33,
   37, 38, 42, 45
privacy 14, 16, 17, 25, 28, 29, 32, 41, 45

six degrees of separation 6, 7
Skype 22
social capital 8, 9
smartphone 5, 12, 13, 38, 44
Strava 31
strong ties 10, 11

tablets 13, 38
tags 18, 19, 30, 32
trolling 35
tweets 24, 25, 40
Twitter 5, 15, 21, 24–25, 40

uploading 14, 19, 20, 28, 29, 45

video 19, 20, 22, 24, 28, 29, 38, 45

weak ties 10, 11
WordPress 31

YouTube 5, 28, 29, 45

Zuckerberg, Mark 22, 23